USBORNE FIRST READING
Level Two

THE STONECUTTER

A folktale from Japan

Retold by Lynne Benton

Illustrated by Lee Cosgrove

Reading consultant: Alison Kelly
Roehampton University

This story
is about a
stonecutter,

a mountain
spirit,

a rich
man,

the sun,

a cloud

and a
mountain.

Once, there was a stonecutter.

He grumbled all day long.

I'm tired.

This stone is too hard.

A mountain spirit
watched him.

My back hurts!

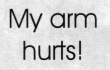

My arm hurts!

One day, a rich man bought some stone.

8

The stonecutter carried
it to his house.

Wow!

"I wish *I* was rich!"
he said.

The mountain spirit smiled...

...and the stonecutter *was* rich.

He sat in his garden
all day, in the sun.

"Whew, it's hot. I wish
I was the sun," he said.

13

The mountain spirit smiled.

And the stonecutter was the sun.

Flowers bloomed and
everyone was happy.

He shone
down.

The flowers turned
brown. Rivers dried up.

"This is no fun," said
the stonecutter sun.

A cloud began to rain.

"I wish *I*
was a cloud,"
said the stonecutter.

18

The
mountain
spirit
smiled.

And the stonecutter
was a cloud.

The stonecutter rained. He couldn't stop raining.

Soon, water covered everything – except the mountain.

"I wish *I* was the mountain," he said.

The mountain spirit smiled again...

The stonecutter liked being the mountain.

Then another stonecutter began to cut chunks off him.

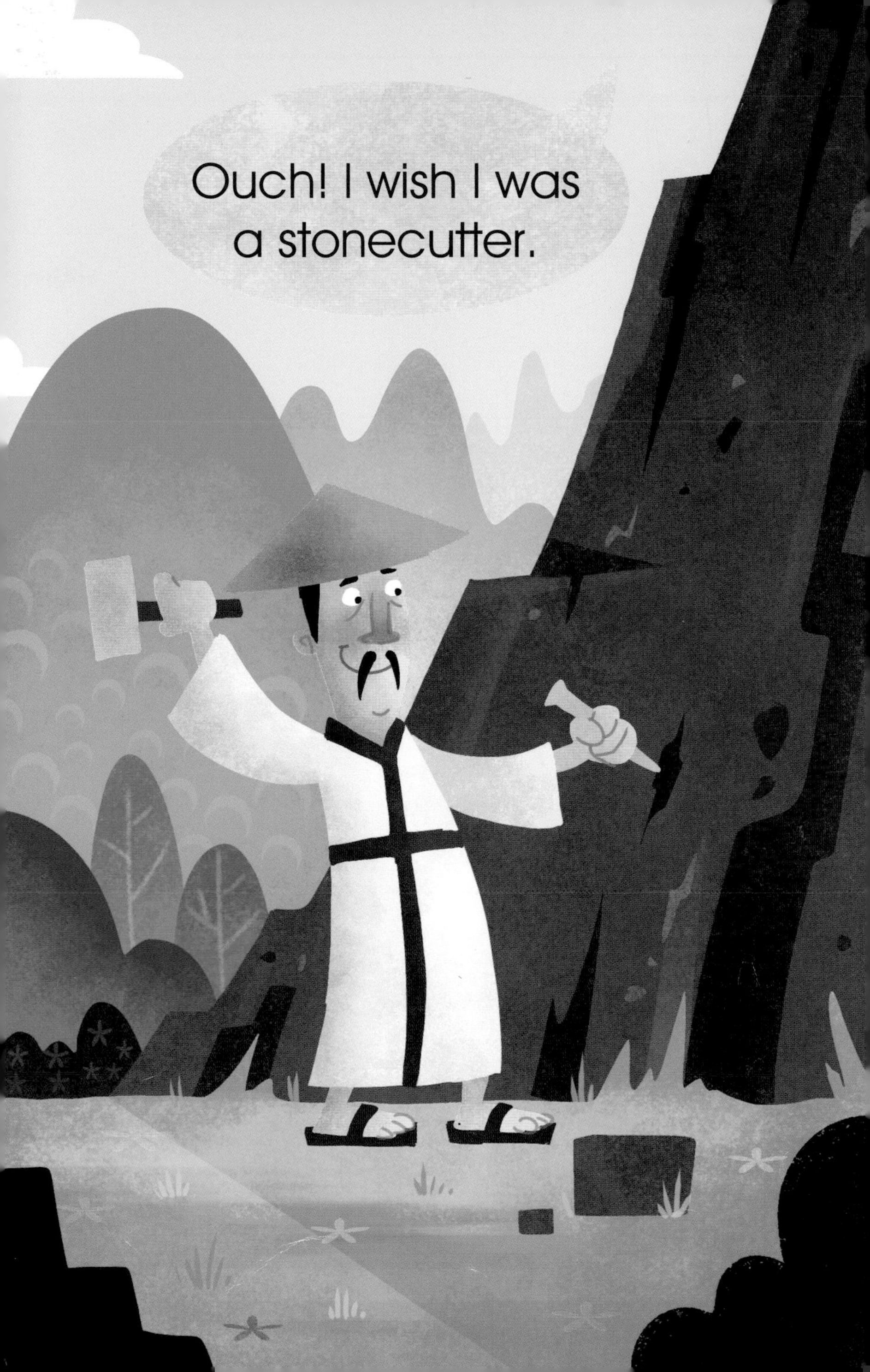
Ouch! I wish I was a stonecutter.

The mountain spirit
smiled one last time.

The stonecutter was
back where he started.

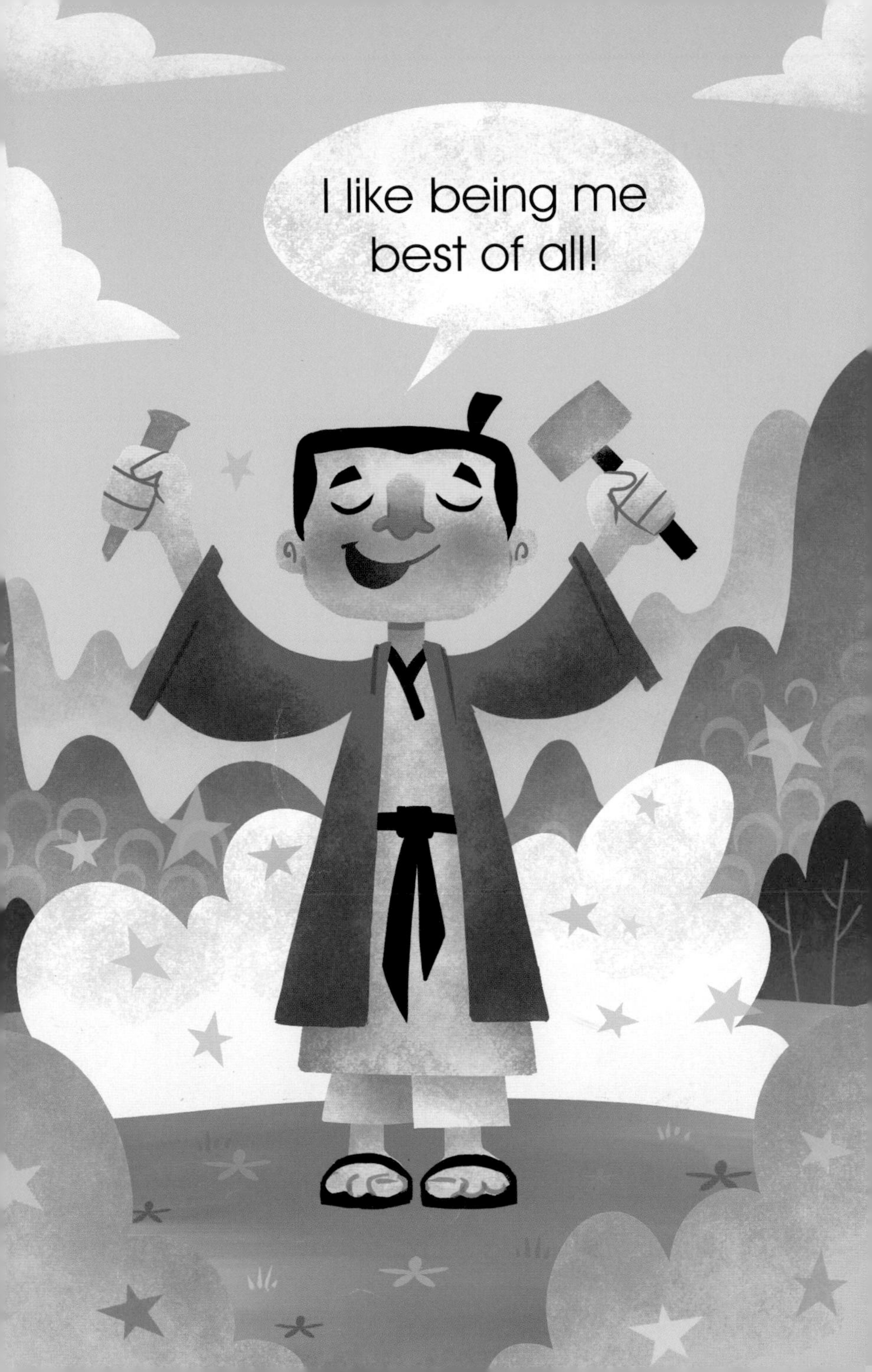
I like being me best of all!

PUZZLES

Puzzle 1

Can you spot the differences between these two pictures?

There are six to find.

Puzzle 2

Choose the best speech bubble for each picture.

Puzzle 3
Find the opposites.

happy

poor

rich

dry

wet

sad

Answers

Puzzle 1

Puzzle 2

This is the life!

Puzzle 3

poor

wet

happy

rich

dry

sad

About The Stonecutter

The Stonecutter is a traditional tale
from Japan. Similar stories
are told in Europe with
different characters,
including a fisherman
and his wife,
and a woman
who lives in a
vinegar bottle.

Designed by Caroline Spatz
Series designer: Russell Punter
Series editor: Lesley Sims

First published in 2009 by Usborne Publishing Ltd., Usborne House,
83-85 Saffron Hill, London EC1N 8RT, England. www.usborne.com
Copyright © 2009 Usborne Publishing Ltd.

USBORNE FIRST READING
Level Three